Collect all the **Apple Bunch Books**

QUALITY BOOKS MADE IN AMERICA

Apple Pie Publishing

Apple Pie Publishing, LLC
P.O. Box 1135
Rockwall, TX 75087
www.applepiepub.com

Book Design by Michael Albee - michaelalbee.com
Author Photo by J. Mathew Butler - jmathewinc.com

The text for this book is set in Optima and Century Gothic. The illustrations in this book are rendered in colored pencil. Manufactured in the U.S.A. with lead free ink and paper.
10 9 8 7 6 5 4 3 2 1

Shapley-Box, Diane.
Tator's Big Race / written and illustrated by Diane
Shapley-Box. -- 1st ed.
p. cm.

SUMMARY: An alligator struggles with never winning. His friends a frog, bird and a rabbit help him realize what is really important.
Audience: Ages 3-7.

LCCN 2010909520
ISBN-13: 978-0-615-38382-8

This book meets or exceeds 2008 CPSIA Section 108 requirements for phthalate content and CPSIA Labeling, Section 103.
Printed at Taylor Specialty Books, Dallas, TX, 1-800-331-8163
Print Run Qty 4M, Date 08/2010

To my husband Kevin, sons Patrick and Mitchell

and to Mom and Dad

Tator's BIG Race

Written and Illustrated by
Diane Shapley-Box

Apple Bunch
Books

Apple Pie Publishing
Rockwall, TX

Near a pond lined with apple trees you will find

Tator the Gator who is thoughtful and kind.

He usually smiled a wide, crooked grin

that stretched from his snout and down to his chin.

Today was different. Today he felt bad.

Today, Tator the Gator looked rather sad.

The Applefest would come every year in the fall.
He would go with his friends. He would go with them all.

He would enter contests, but his friends always won.

They had ribbons and trophies, but Tator had none.

Tator tried to win the pie contest.

He baked and baked with little rest.

But Perdie the Birdie, his good friend,

was always the winner in the end.

Tator tried to win the juggling event
that was always held in the big, striped tent.
But Cabbit the Rabbit, a juggling clown,
would end up wearing the champion's crown.

Tator tried to win the applesauce contest.

He tried many recipes. He gave it his best.

But his little green pal, a frog named Fred,

would win the star all shiny and red.

Tator the Gator explained with a frown,
"I have never won a ribbon or crown.
I have no talents, and I am lacking skills.
I have nothing to put on my windowsills."

Tator's tears tumbled and fell to the floor.

He lowered his head and ran out the door.

That night his friends met in the yard.

Fred said, "We must think very hard.

Maybe there's something that Tator could do.

Maybe there's a hint or maybe a clue."

Fred saw a poster nailed to a tree.

He pulled it off for the others to see.

"It's a race to see how fast you can run.

We can train Tator. This will be fun."

With rubber from a tire and an old shoelace,

together they made shoes for Tator's big race.

Fred found a whistle that he could blow

to signal Tator when he should go.

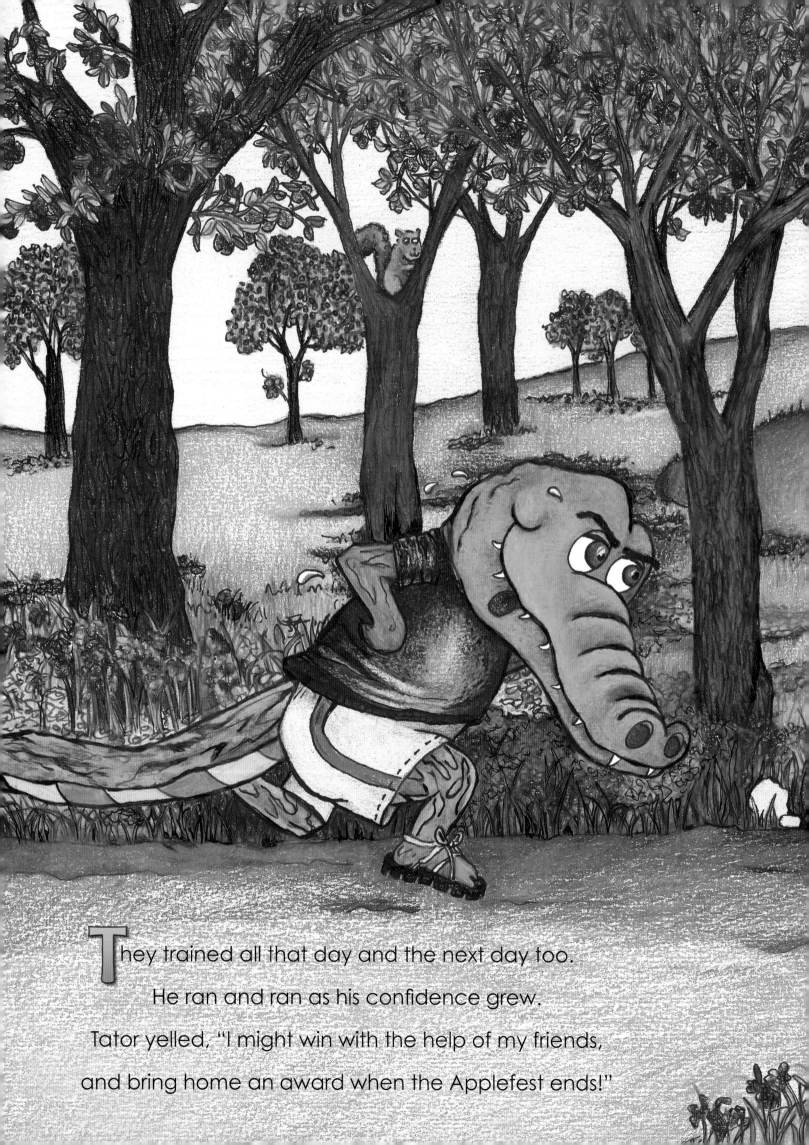

They trained all that day and the next day too.

He ran and ran as his confidence grew.

Tator yelled, "I might win with the help of my friends,

and bring home an award when the Applefest ends!"

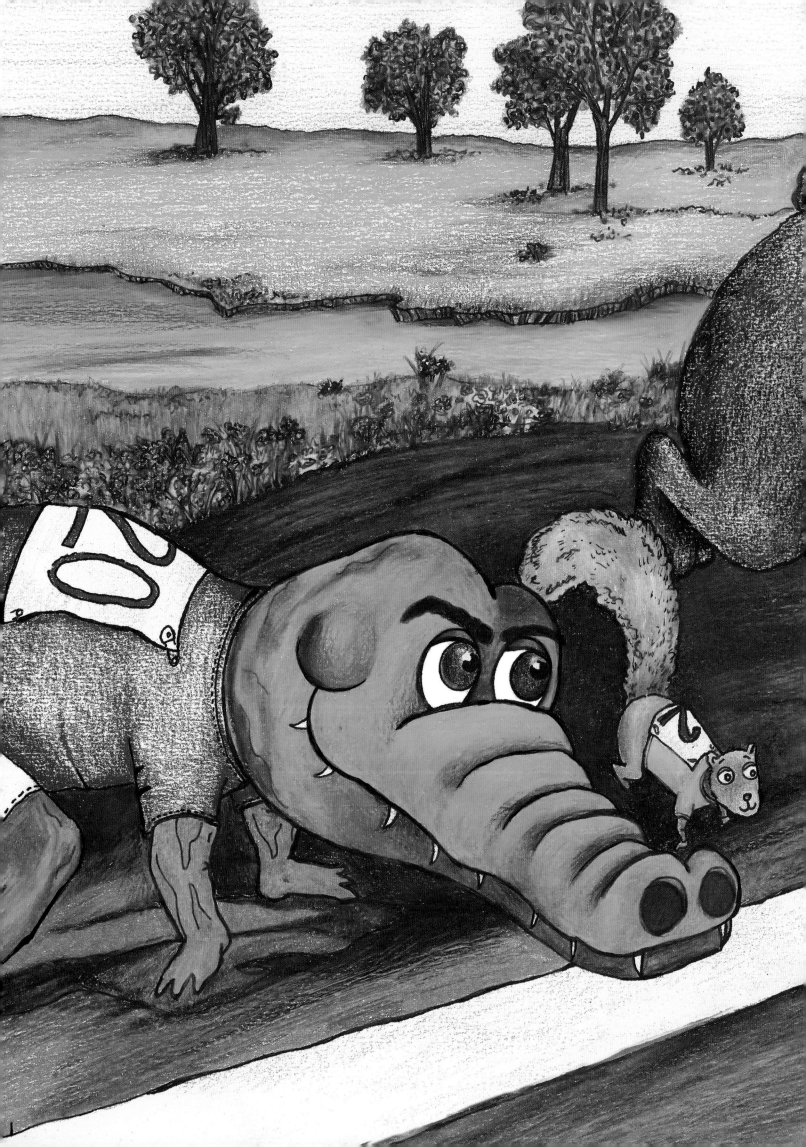

Applefest arrived the very next day.

Tator was excited and led the way.

He lined up for the race with his knees bent.

When the whistle blew, like a flash he went.

"Run, Tator, Run!" Perdie let out a yell.

"Go, Tator, Go!" Cabbit called out as well.

Fred climbed up on a branch so he could see.

He jumped up and down and cheered happily.

Fred slipped and he flipped and down he fell.

He dropped from the branch and let out a yell!

Tator was just about to win the race

when he spotted his friend's terrified face.

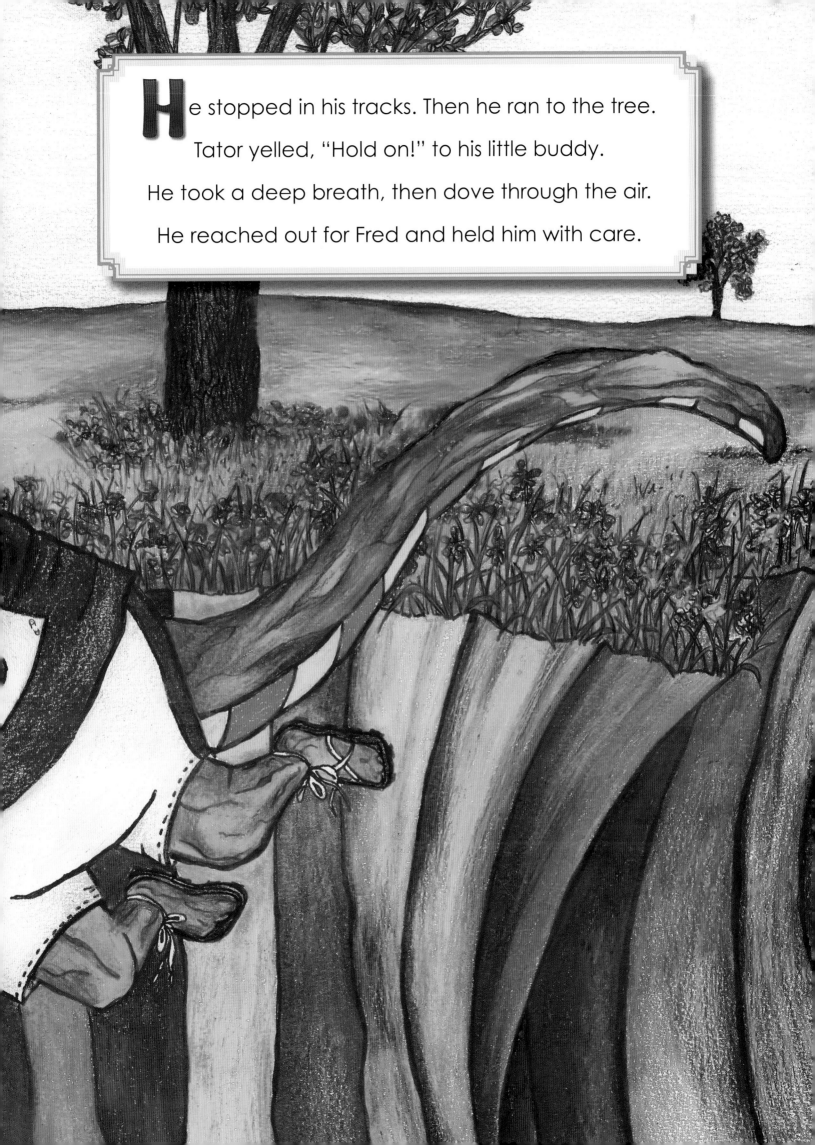

He stopped in his tracks. Then he ran to the tree.

Tator yelled, "Hold on!" to his little buddy.

He took a deep breath, then dove through the air.

He reached out for Fred and held him with care.

Tator placed his friend safely on the ground.

Everyone watched without making a sound.

Everyone thought it. It was too sad to say.

Tator lost the race. He lost again today. 20

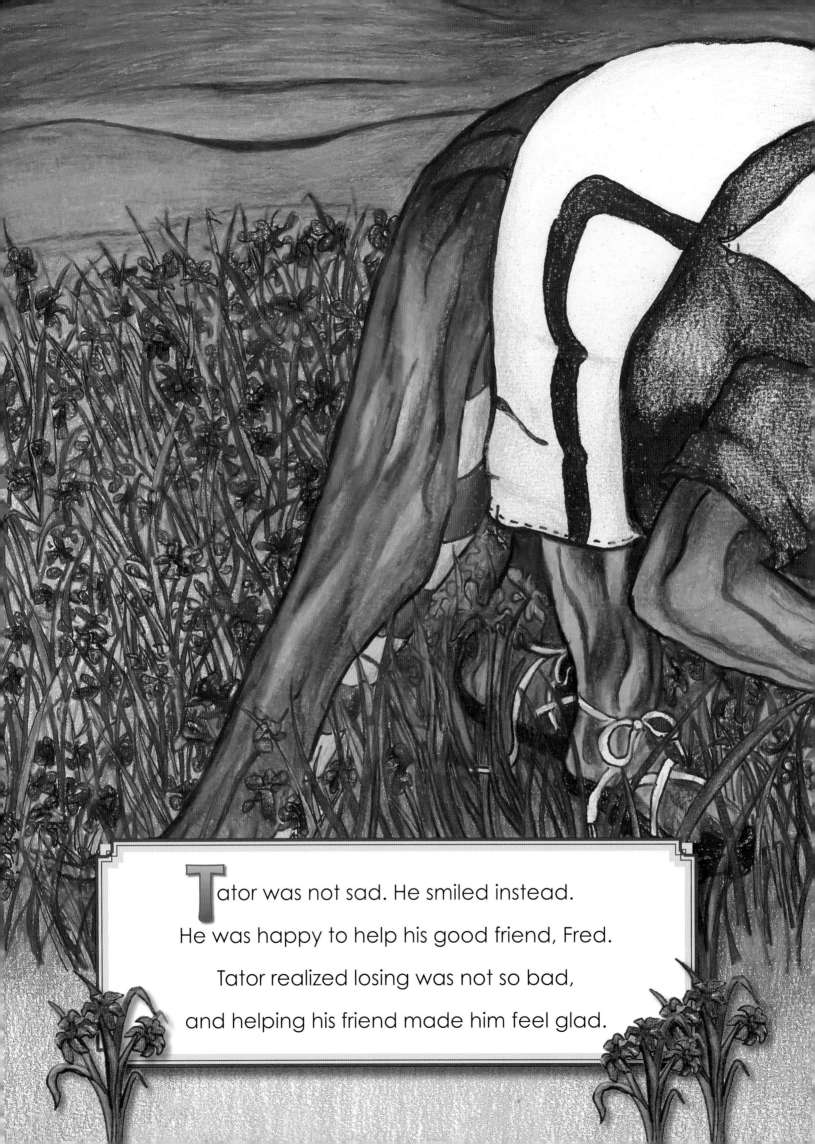

Tator was not sad. He smiled instead.

He was happy to help his good friend, Fred.

Tator realized losing was not so bad,

and helping his friend made him feel glad.

Applefest was over. It had come to an end.

Tator had proven he was a very good friend.

An award did not matter like it had before.

Yet Tator was thrilled when he opened his door.

His friends brought a trophy, shiny and gold,

with "**THE BEST FRIEND EVER**" written in bold.

The End

Apple Facts

Apples come in many shades of reds, greens, and yellows.

An average apple has 5 apple tree seeds in it.

Apples float in water.

Apples can be as small as cherries and as large as grapefruits.

QUALITY BOOKS
MADE IN AMERICA

Apple Pie Publishing, LLC

Apple Pie Publishing, LLC is dedicated to bringing quality American made books and products to their readers. All books are printed in the USA on quality lead free paper & ink.

Apple Pie Publishing, LLC is active in the community and an avid supporter for medical research and fundraising. The Apple Bunch Book series has donated thousands of dollars with the first book *Apples for Fred*. A percentage of all the profits made by Apple Pie Publishing, LLC is dedicated to local and national charities.

To find out more about Apple Pie Publishing, LLC and all of the Apple Bunch Books please visit:

www.applepiepub.com

Diane Shapley-Box
Author & Illustrator

Diane is an award winning artist and a graduate of The Art Institute of Dallas. She has worked as a professional artist and a concept designer. Her work has been featured in magazines, books and newspapers. Her first book *Apples for Fred* from the Apple Bunch Book series has received rave reviews from parents, teachers and children.

• • • • • • • • • • • • • • • •

Learn more about Diane and her books at
www.applepiepub.com.

Collect all the
Apple Bunch Books

QUALITY BOOKS MADE IN AMERICA

Autographed Apple Bunch Books
gift packs available.

Visit **www.applepiepub.com** for details.

Special thanks to:

Weymon and Ann Box
Kathleen Feigen
Judith Shapley
Michael Albee